The WOLF and the SHIELD

An Adventure with Saint Patrick

By Sherry Weaver Smith

Pauline
BOOKS & MEDIA
Boston

Library of Congress Cataloging-in-Publication Data

Names: Smith, Sherry, 1969- | McNally, Nicholas, illustrator.
Title: The wolf and the shield : an adventure with Saint Patrick / written by
  Sherry Weaver Smith ; illustrated by Nicholas McNally.
Description: Boston, MA : Pauline Books & Media, [2016] | Summary: "A
  young boy is influenced by his friendship with St. Patrick and his
  experiences caring for an orphan wolf pup"-- Provided by publisher.
Identifiers: LCCN 2015027479 (print) | LCCN 2015036936 (ebook) | ISBN
  9780819883568 (pbk.) | ISBN 0819883565 (pbk.) | ISBN 9780819883575
  (epub) | ISBN 9780819883582 (mobi) | ISBN 9780819883599 (pdf)
Subjects: LCSH: Patrick, Saint, 373?-463?--Juvenile fiction. | CYAC: Patrick,
  Saint, 373?-463?--Fiction. | Wolves--Fiction. | Orphaned animals--Fiction.
  | Wildlife rescue--Fiction. | Human-animal relationships--Fiction. |
  Christian life--Fiction.
Classification: LCC PZ7.1.S656 Wo 2016 (print) | LCC PZ7.1.S656 (ebook) |
  DDC
  [Fic]--dc23
LC record available at http://lccn.loc.gov/2015027479

This is a novelized story including Saint Patrick. While Saint Patrick is a real
historical figure, elements of this story—including other characters,
conversations, the plot, and events—are fictional products of the author's
imagination.

"P" and PAULINE are registered trademarks of the Daughters of Saint Paul.

Cover/book design by Mary Joseph Peterson, FSP & Putri Mamesah,
(Novice, Daughters of St. Paul)

Published by Pauline Books & Media, 50 Saint Paul's Avenue, Boston, MA
02130-3491

Printed in the U.S.A.

WATS VSAUSAPEOILL9-110051 8356-5

www.pauline.org

Pauline Books & Media is the publishing house of the Daughters of Saint
Paul, an international congregation of women religious serving the Church
with the communications media.

1 2 3 4 5 6 7 8 9   20 19 18 17 16

To my daughter, Laura Joan Smith,
and to my inspirations for this story:
Michael Gordon Ross Smith,
Declan Denis Samuelson,
and especially my father,
Kelly Edward Weaver

CONTENTS

People and Places vi

The Hunt

   1 2

   2 5

   3 8

   4 11

   5 13

   6 16

   7 18

Joining a Pack?

   8 22

   9 26

A Shield of Protection

   10 32

   11 34

   12 37

A Slippery Stumble

   13 42

   14 44

A Slashing Attack

   15 50

   16 52

   17 56

   18 57

A New Den

19 62

20 64

21 67

22 72

The Forest

23 78

24 81

Betrayal

25 86

26 88

27 90

28 93

The Saint's Path

29 98

30 100

The Lake

31 104

32 106

33 109

Historical Note 114

Saint Patrick's Prayer 115

Discussion Questions 116

Acknowledgments 118

people and places

Who you will meet in this story

Kieran (KEER-ahn)
> An eleven-year-old boy living in Ireland who has been trying to care for his family since his father died two years earlier.

Patrick
> A Catholic Christian priest and bishop who has traveled from the island of Britain to share his faith with people in Ireland.

Aisling (ASH-ling)
> An orphaned wolf pup.

Kieran's mother
> A widow whose husband died two years earlier and mother of Kieran and Riordan.

Riordan (REER-dan)
> Kieran's six-year-old brother.

Ida (EE-dah)
> A ten-year-old girl who is Kieran's and Riordan's friend.

Alby (ALL-bay)

>Ida's eleven-year-old brother.

Carrick

>The leader of the clan king's warriors who protect Kieran's group of families and their farms.

Where and when this story takes place

This story takes place on the island of Ireland in the fifth century. The places in this story are part of today's Northern Ireland, near the city of Armagh (ar-MAH).

What you will encounter in this story

Bog

>A wetland with a mix of grassy land, muddy land, and small ponds.

Clan

>A group of families forming a community with its own chieftain or king.

Elver

>A baby eel.

Foster family

> In Ireland during the fifth century, many children lived with families other than their own to build strong friendships within the clan. Children still saw their birth parents.

Gorse

> A bush with yellow flowers.

Ogham (AW-gum)

> A very old alphabet used for the Irish language, often found on stone monuments.

Shillelagh (sheh-LAY-lee)

> A club made from a tree branch, often used for a weapon or sometimes in sports.

Sett

> The home, or burrow, of a badger.

Torc

> A U-shaped, metal necklace worn by important people.

THE HUNT

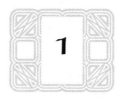

1

Kieran searched the shadows for the trail showing which way to go. The far-off tree line blurred into a smoky smudge like the arch of a wolf's back. The moonlight sunk through the forest leaves and fell down, lost among the roots. The boy turned, his elbows bent like spiky wood branches.

He heard the shouts of the big group of hunters. He wouldn't go with them. They'd scare off the wolves with their arguing and boasting. In silence, with one spear, he planned to kill a wolf by himself. A pack of them had killed another family's cow. His family wasn't rich and had only one young cow, so Kieran didn't care much about guarding cattle against wolves. What he did want was the prize of killing a wolf. Everyone would respect him then, no matter whether his family had lots of cows or not. In Ireland, protecting families and their food was what mattered most.

Kieran listened. Was that a howl or just men shouting to each other? He led with his spear. He would have only one throw. Maybe that's all he would need. After all, hadn't Carrick, the clan king's best warrior, praised Kieran's aim?

His foot cracked a twig as he bent to go under a tree branch. He looked up to the moon, but a shadow cloaked it. Something had stepped over him, and he drew his spear back.

"Peace be with you. Put your weapon down," said the shape. "Did you hear the howling call through the oak trees?"

Kieran had never heard the man's voice before. And his question made no sense to him. "I'm on a hunt. I've got to pass," said Kieran.

"What are you hunting for?"

"A wolf," said Kieran as he tried to slip round the man who still stood in front of him. "A pack attacked a cow at a farm nearby. I must pass."

"But what does your heart hunt for?" The man lowered his hood, showing his face. Even in the dim light, Kieran could see his blue eyes. The man lifted his hand to a white blossom on one of the trees. "Go to the crescent meadow," he said. "You will find what you hunt for there." And with that strange command, the man stepped away.

The crescent meadow was deeper in the forest. Some said the trees that used to stand there had been cleared away by a giant who had been gathering firewood. Kieran wasn't sure how to find it and wondered whether or not to try. The man hadn't

seemed to understand, but maybe he had seen the wolf there. So he started under the white blossom, finding one path and then another, until he came to a crescent-shaped meadow.

Coming out to the moon-white grass, Kieran fell to his knees to look around. Tiny, cuplike flowers glowed in bell shapes and seemed to ring. No, the sound was something else. Loosening his hold on his spear, he crawled.

A squeaking noise came from a low rise at the edge of the meadow. As he got closer, he saw a hole large enough for him to fit through. *Squeak, squeak.* The edges of the hole changed shape, like smoke rising from a fire. Kieran realized that there must be an animal there. Moving from side to side, it made the edges of the hole seem blurry. Kieran squinted. The pale gray of the animal became clearer. A wolf. A wolf pup.

2

"The wolf's den!" Kieran was surprised he'd said it aloud. The little wolf scrambled into the hole.

Now what? Should he go in? If the wolf pack was out hunting, he could kill the pup and still get a small reward. But what if the pack was resting inside? The squeaking tempted him, and, on quick and quiet feet, Kieran rushed to the hole.

He had to squeeze to get his shoulders through the entryway, but then he slid fast. There wasn't enough time to even think to jab a knife in the floor to stop himself. The moonlight was gone.

A small growl sounded, not so far away. Kieran pulled his feet further in. The skin above his boots felt cold, a target for a wolf that could be following him. What if he got stuck and the pack should return?

Curving into a shell shape, Kieran slithered. He could see a tiny glint of teeth. The pup had gone up to a sloping ledge. The den was bigger inside, but he still couldn't draw back his spear. His knife in its scabbard had twisted around onto his back.

Kieran put one hand in a leather glove he carried and pushed toward the teeth. The pup didn't rush toward his hand as he expected. Instead, it froze like a rabbit in a field. Keeping his one hand in front of the pup's blunt nose, with his other hand he grabbed the back of the pup's neck.

Now he had a new problem: how to get out of the den with the twisting and growling pup held against him. The spear's shaft scraped against the den's ceiling. Kieran felt a bite tear into his cloak, but he kept his grip strong. Finally, he could see the entrance again.

Back in the moonlight, Kieran held the pup away from his chest. Its furry feet fell just down past his elbow. With one hand, he would have to tether it somehow. That way he could thrust in the spear. He unhooked a rope from his waist and looped it over the pup's thrashing head and biting teeth.

As he tightened the rope, he felt the pup's fur, soft as dandelion fluff drifting over a meadow in late summer. He paused. "Dandelion fluff," that was something Ida, a girl he knew, would think.

He put the pup on the ground and stomped his foot on the rope. *You won't get away*, he thought. The creature stumbled to bite his leg. He grabbed the pup with one hand and kept his foot on the rope. With the pup lunging and biting, he couldn't line up the spear. So with his other hand, Kieran stretched to grab a heavy slab of quartz. He slapped it down on the end of the rope to hold it in place.

"What does your heart hunt for?" The strange question from the man he'd met came into his mind. It kept echoing there and wouldn't stop. *I am a hunter*, he thought.

In a motion he'd done so many times, he drew back the spear. The pup ran in circles—growling, then whimpering; charging, then cowering.

Kieran focused and aimed, the last things to do before striking. The pup's blue eyes looked straight at him. Kieran could see the golden amber they would become, and the fear they would bring to his whole clan. A sky and a sun, those colors, shone both at once.

But Kieran could not bring himself to kill the pup. He loosened his fingers, let the spear fall to his side, and sunk to the ground.

3

Kieran yanked the tether from under the rock and shoved the pup into a leather rucksack he carried. Avoiding the soft fur, he used a knife to cut a few air holes. The bag was ruined. And for what?

Kieran tucked the bag under his cloak. His mother had made him wear it for protection against the damp air, and it could be a blanket if he should ever get lost. He held the bag in the crook of his arm as the pup continued to shift.

The boy paused to think. He should toss the pup over his shoulder and leave it where it fell. A wolf pup would only grow into a wolf as surely as summer turned into winter. But Kieran could still hear the man's question: What did his heart hunt for?

Kieran ran, but he still couldn't decide what to do. He hadn't felt the pup move in some time. What if there wasn't enough air for it? He supposed then that would be the end of it. *No more worries.* But as he thought this, a memory of his father tucking a blanket around him flashed into his mind. There wasn't any time for memories. Kieran kept running out of the forest.

Shouts sounded as loud as shovels hitting cold stone.

"It was *my* spear."

"No, *mine*! Don't you see the three notches?"

So many voices clamored that Kieran could barely distinguish the men's voices from the boys'. It didn't matter. None was his father's. He had died two years before, when Kieran was nine. Now Kieran took care of his family.

He stepped out of the shadows, but his almost-black hair and dark clothing blended with the darkness, and no one saw him.

The biggest man carried a dead wolf. *A dead she-wolf,* Kieran guessed. Her paws would never again run along paths in the grass.

If he spoke up, he could still have some of the prize. He had the she-wolf's pup, helplessly hanging from his shoulder. He could show it right there. How would it survive anyway with its mother dead?

As the men and boys argued, a dark pool formed on the ground below the wolf's shape. In the daytime, that spot would be as red as rowan berries. From the crook of Kieran's elbow came a soft squeak. But the mother wolf couldn't hear, and her dead eyes were as empty as caves.

Something inside, maybe Kieran's heart, told him to run. His chest burned as he fled away fast. He knew that if the hunters saw him, they might throw their spears. It had become so dark, they might not be able to see that he was a boy.

Kieran didn't have a shield to protect himself or the pup. His father's old one was broken, and he couldn't bear to fix it. He had run back to the battlefield where his father had been killed to find it. He hadn't wanted the enemy clan to steal it. But no one was there—only the broken shield and ravens, the black birds that came for dead things.

He kept running, fast like warriors led by Carrick. He dreamed that someday he, too, would become one of those warriors. He made it safely to the edge of the woods near his family's small hut.

Where should he leave the wolf pup? Outside alone? But what if it howled? All the men were still looking for wolves.

But what if the pack came to find it? What if wolves then attacked his family's farm and killed Kieran's gentle calf? He thought of the calf's round eyes that turned to look at him wherever he went.

He'd saved the pup once and he'd saved it again by running away. Kieran decided to keep the pup quiet overnight. He needed time to think it through. He would have to choose what to do in the morning.

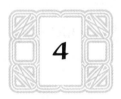

4

Kieran made a little collar out of rope and tethered the pup to a sapling at the edge of the forest. The pup pulled against the rope for a moment and turned to try to bite it, but its young snout was too short. Although its teeth flashed silver, they were still small.

As he was about to settle next to the pup, Kieran heard his mother calling him. At the sound of her voice, the pup chewed on the rope and seemed more awake than ever. *Quiet,* he thought.

He stepped toward the house, shaped like a beehive. Since his father had died, it seemed that the house leaned to the side, like a tree that had lost some roots. He stepped through the doorway.

"You're safe. I was worried," his mother said. His younger brother settled back to sleep.

"They got the wolf," Kieran said. "I saw it slung over a hunter's shoulder."

"Just one?" his mother asked. "But there are more. They said they heard a whole pack."

"It's likely the others were scared off," Kieran said.

"Evil animals," said his mother. "You were brave to help your uncle and protect our calf." The clan king had a law that each family group, all the men related to one grandfather, had to hunt wolves each week.

"I didn't want to help him." Kieran's uncle did the right thing and helped his dead brother's family. But to Kieran, his uncle could never take the place of his father. That is why the boy never wanted to spend much time with him.

Kieran stretched out on his cot, leather straps held by oak planks. *Don't howl,* he willed the pup. He was relieved to hear only his own stomach growling.

"Kieran . . ."

He turned away from his mother.

The fire was dying. Kieran's mother tended the hearth. She swept the ashes into three even piles, all in a circle. She laid thin strips of sod among the smoky piles. She covered the whole circle with more ash. She said a quiet prayer to keep the embers warm for the next morning's fire. Kieran thought he heard her say a new word: "Jesus."

When his mother fell asleep, he crept back out to the wolf pup. It snapped awake as he stepped near.

Kieran didn't meet its eyes. Instead, he dropped low to comfort it—like another pup. Out here, he would know in a moment if the pup tried to howl.

5

The cold morning's damp seeped through Kieran's cloak. Everything felt chilly except his arm—because in his arm was the warmth of the pup, curled up with its tail wrapped around its nose.

"Why aren't you afraid?" he whispered. "Do you like me? You're probably just trying to keep warm. Are you all right?" Kieran's heart beat more than he expected when it stayed quiet. He petted the pup, and it wiggled awake. He was surprised that he was relieved.

Now Kieran could see the pup in the light of day. It had light gray fur like birch tree trunks mixed with the soft white of a snowy path on the way to an adventure.

It was a girl pup. He thought about naming her Aisling, but thought again. No, her name should be "Reward." He could still turn her in.

A weak ray of sun came through the spring leaves, and the pup whimpered. She didn't fight the tether or Kieran. A wild thing should be rushing into something wild. *She must be too weak to run away,* he thought. He must hunt her some food, maybe a rabbit. But he had left his spear inside the house.

Kieran crossed the meadow. In the vegetable garden the straight leaves of onions looked like spearheads. He smoothed the tunic he wore under his cloak. His mother had woven and dyed it with gray and yellow squares lined up together like a stone wall pattern. The woolen trousers he wore were loose and too short.

He could hear his brother laughing. His mother always said that it seemed as if her two sons came from different valleys. Only six years old, Riordan was always bending grass into animals or pretending rocks were people. But to Kieran, rocks were good for building a wall or hurling at something they might eat for dinner.

As he made his way to the corner of their small hut, Riordan became quiet. This was the starting signal of one of his silly games.

"Boo!" shouted out a small figure, disguised as something woodsy. A small tree seemed to be growing out of his back.

"Riordan, what now?"

Riordan wildly danced and turned around. Two oak branches stuck out from the back of his tunic. The leaves bent down toward his messy hair. "I'm the wild Green Man."

"No, you're my brother who should be doing his chores now—like weeding the vegetable garden. How did you get those branches there anyway?" Kieran reached to grab them out, but his brother ducked. *One day, he would be good at hunting and fighting*, Kieran thought, *if he could get all the stories out of his head.*

"Ida put them there."

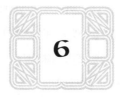

6

"Ida?" Her hair was gold like the sunrise and she had a sun-round face. Kieran felt that he wanted to see her and run back to the forest and hide from her at the same time. "Is she still here?" he asked.

But Riordan was twirling around again. Never a straight story out of him. The answer came from the door to his house.

"Kieran, it's a fine morning. How are you?" asked Ida.

"Fine enough. Busy," said Kieran.

Riordan grabbed the girl's hands. The two began spinning. Kieran went past, into the house, mumbled a greeting to his mother, and grabbed his spear and dagger.

"Ida brought us some extra mutton her brothers butchered," his mother said, while she ground some grain.

"I can hunt enough for us. We don't need it," Kieran said with too much pride, but in his heart he felt that the sheep meat would help feed the little pup in the forest.

"They have more men to help in their family. She has four brothers and their father . . ."

"Their father is still alive. I know." Kieran grabbed the parcel and brushed past his mother.

Then he thought of the pup. Like wolves running single file, his words came out stronger than he expected. "Thank you, Ida. This mutton is a help."

"You are so welcome." Her smile was bright. "Later, your mother and Riordan and I are going to see a man called Patrick. Maybe you could come with us to the church. He is a priest, a leader. Patrick tells us stories about Jesus, about how he loves us from heaven and is all around us. We'll get back before sunset . . ." She touched a small twig cross she'd made to wear around her neck.

"Perhaps," he said, trying to be polite. "But I don't know how this Patrick or his stories could help me." Kieran shrugged. "And I can only go if Carrick, the warrior, isn't here. He will be looking for the boy who has the best aim with his spear."

"But *I* know how Patrick can help you. Patrick has strong shields!"

"Shields? But does he give them away?"

"Yes, he gives people shields to protect them."

"I'd like a new wood shield with leather. One that would work." Kieran said. Then he wouldn't have to face fixing his father's old one. It hadn't saved his father's life. How could he rely on it now? And a shield was becoming more important, at least as long as he was deciding what to do about the wolf pup. "But why would anyone give a shield away for nothing? This Patrick must want something in return."

Carrick would want something, he thought.

"Will you at least go and listen?"

"For a chance at a new shield? Yes."

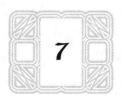

7

Kieran could hear his mother calling to him, but he ran away from the house and through the meadow anyway. He ducked under the branches of the trees at the break to the forest. He saw the wolf pup stumble to her feet, almost as if her body was too big for her. This time she growled, but as he unwrapped a bit of the mutton Ida had brought, the pup forgot her fear and came forward. She lowered her head and crept so that her belly bent the grass in a path toward Kieran.

When the pup tried to gnaw off some of the meat, her teeth weren't sharp enough to pull it away from the bone. She whimpered. Kieran realized she might not be old enough to eat it. He began to pull the meat away from her, but the pup took it as a game. She growled as her short tail wagged. Kieran laughed. He tickled her tummy and she turned on her back, still holding the bit of meat. He gave it a sharper tug and got it out of her reach. He chopped at the meat with his knife and was glad when he saw she could eat the smaller pieces.

When the pup finished, she wagged her tail and leapt onto the fleece wrapping. She grasped it in her mouth and shook it all around.

Kieran had to laugh. "So you think you're a good hunter?" Kieran tugged a bit on the free end. The wolf pup bent her head and growled just as he had seen some pet dogs do. He copied her, bending his head and growling, and they played tug-of-war with the fleece.

"Maybe one day we could hunt together?" But he felt a little sad as he said it. The last time he'd had fun hunting was with his father. Still, with a wolf pup, he wouldn't be so lonely . . .

Soon, as with all young animals, the energy flowed out of her like a thin stream on a hill. She dropped back down to the ground with half-closed eyes.

"Maybe I could pet you now? So what if I get nipped." Kieran held out his hand to her nose first. She sniffed and nuzzled his palm. He went to rub her head between her ears. "Aisling, you don't even look so much like a wolf with the tips of your ears curled down." He smiled. He'd said her name out loud. That settled it. Her name was Aisling.

As Aisling slept, he watched her belly rise and fall with each breath. The boy and wolf pup were so still that even a mouse ventured out, then turned right back to where it came from. Maybe to a nest.

"I need a wide shield to protect us both," he said to her. "I'm not sure how, but I'm going to keep you."

JOINING A PACK?

8

Kieran's feet pointed east toward the sunrise as he slept. That's the way they'd buried his father. Something bumping against the side of his bed woke him.

"Riordan," Kieran turned to the floor, "what are you doing?"

"Hiding," Riordan said in a shaky voice, his blond curls dulled in the dimness. Dogs barked in the distance.

"Carrick must be here," said Kieran, swinging out of bed. He grabbed his cloak and spear. His heart beat in time with the dogs barking. He wasn't afraid of Carrick, but he was afraid that the dogs might find Aisling. He wished he had time to check on her, but he had to hurry.

In front of a rundown house, a woman was handing over some barley bread to one of Carrick's men. Kieran wondered why he would go to get bread there. The warrior shoved her. Surely, the king wouldn't want Carrick or his men doing that. Kieran felt uneasy, but shrugged his shoulders. He should think only about throwing his spear. Boys were scrambling out of their huts and all of them would want to look sharp. Carrick would not be easy to impress. Kieran had heard that Carrick could even hit a fast-moving chariot with a spear.

In the center of the group, the warrior, Carrick, stood tall and regal. He wore a metal torc, a U-shaped necklace, around his neck. The torc showed that he was a favorite of the clan king who ruled the land where Kieran lived.

The warrior had a sharp falcon face, an ale-soaked mustache, and auburn wavy hair. He was armed with a long sword held in a leather belt. No one dared to approach as he swung around a shille-lagh, a blackthorn club cured and polished to be as shiny as raven wings.

In the cold Irish morning on a pale spring day, Carrick's arms were bare. Kieran wished he hadn't worn his cloak. Some of Carrick's warriors were hammering stakes into the ground. Kieran tapped his spear in the dirt over and over. He wanted to have his chance. It wouldn't be long.

"I am here to see who has the best aim with a spear. It's that simple. I will be back to take only the best," Carrick said in a voice like rocks falling against each other. "Our warriors bring honor to our king. We steal cattle from enemy clans so our clan will become even richer. We protect the borders so that

no enemies will come here. Since I've been in charge, not one cow of ours, *not one,* has been stolen!" He marched over to the boys and spoke to Kieran first.

"You," Carrick said, "you, with the dark hair. Go."

The men almost had no time to move from the stakes. Kieran drew a sharp breath in. On the top of each stake was a misty-colored tuft of fur.

"Go!" Carrick cuffed the back of Kieran's head. Kieran didn't let his head bow forward. "In battle, you can't stand and stare."

"Right." *Don't think. Just aim it,* he thought. He drew back his spear as he pulled all of his feelings deep inside him. He hurled it as the other boys looked on. As the point divided the air, it seemed as if it was making its own choice. Kieran thought of how things took their own way after you made the decision to let go of them.

His spear found its mark—a clean slice into the fur, a heart broken in two.

"Good," Carrick said. "Mark him down. The dark-haired one."

Another man said, "He's a widow's son, though. His father's dead. You know the saying: 'Widow's sons don't take orders.' No discipline."

Kieran glared toward the man speaking.

Carrick said, "I care only about his aim. Mark him down."

9

Kieran made sure not to appear to pay too much attention to the other boys' attempts. These sons of free farmers, "cowmen" who had cattle, had a duty to fight as warriors for the clan king. But it seemed Carrick would only pick a few, the best.

Ida's brother, Alby, was one year older than she was and the same age as Kieran. Kieran watched out of the corner of his eye as Alby stepped up. He had the same sunrise-colored hair as his sister, but not much of her grace. Alby's hands were big, his fingers wide like roots, his steps plodding like a forest giant. His spear wasn't straight as he pulled it back. It wobbled after he let it go. It was no surprise that it missed the target by a cow's width. At least Ida wasn't there to see it.

As other boys threw, Alby whispered to Kieran, "I don't want Carrick to pick me. I missed on purpose."

"What about your duty to the king[...] you're making up a story to cover up y[...] Kieran said.

"I've been spending time at the chu[...] Patrick. Just like Ida has. I'm not sure about Carrick. I've heard that his men steal food. Do you think that's what the king wants? Do you think that's right?"

Kieran clenched his fists. "They take cattle from enemy clans! Clans like the one that killed my father!" *How dare Alby tell stories when he couldn't even hit the side of a hut with his spear!*

Carrick approached Kieran. "You are the only one we want. We'll be back for you."

Kieran stood taller. "It would be an honor," he said, but Carrick and his men were already walking away.

Kieran was proud that he would serve as a warrior. Maybe they would even raid another king's cattle, and he would get a share. Kieran could get a cow to add to the one they had. That would really help his mother. *If only Riordan would be better about his chores,* he thought. *But that boy's head is too full of stories.*

But what about the wolf pup? If he joined Carrick's men, he wouldn't be able to keep it. Kieran alked back out to the stake to yank the jagged spearhead out of the animal fur. Now so close to it, he could see how it matched the color of Aisling's coat. Feeling sick, he touched the fur, his fingers tracing down a trickle of blood. The wound was still wet, maybe not even one hour old. Kieran turned to see the backs of Carrick and his men riding away on their horses. He felt the dry taste of dread in his mouth. *Did Carrick and his men find Aisling in the forest?* He wondered. *Or was the fur from a different wolf pup?*

"Lucky throw," some of the boys called to him out jealously. But Kieran was already running. *I was only thinking about looking good for Carrick. But what if I actually pierced Aisling's fur with my own spear?* That thought stunned him. Kieran couldn't even see the trees in front of him as he pushed his legs to move even faster. *Just let her be all right.*

The place he had left the pup was still full of late morning shadows. His eyes strained to see. But one shadow stood up and wagged its tail—Aisling. Sadness left him as fast as a wild wind blowing through moorland grass. He wanted to rush toward her and gather her up, but something he saw made him think better of it. He paused and dropped down to the ground slowly.

The pup sniffed all around. Her ears went back and forth as she curiously listened to something before she ran, stumbling toward a ring of trees. Soon Kieran heard it too—a rabbit scratching.

Kieran killed it, gave Aisling some of its meat, and packed up the rest for his family. Glancing at the pup one last time before he left, he worried that the tether might be too tight around her neck. So he loosened it a bit and headed home.

a shield
of
protection

10

As Kieran rushed through the rest of his chores, he kept thinking about Patrick. As a warrior, he would need a new shield. Would Ida remember to stop by? Maybe she hadn't really meant for him to go.

But Ida did stop, and Kieran's mother and Riordan came along. Kieran was surprised to see an already worn path. He knew that Ida, his mother, and Riordan had been to the church before. Ida had told him she'd been baptized, something about water that meant she was a follower of Jesus.

"Moo," said Riordan. "I see a cow in the sky."

"No such thing," said Kieran bluntly.

"Don't you see the cloud over there mooing toward us?" Ida asked. "And the sheep behind?"

"If I look at the ridge, maybe," Kieran said. Ida tapped him on the arm. He felt both embarrassed and happy.

"I'm going to catch it!" Riordan jumped straight up. For once, Kieran was happy about his brother's fanciful ways. It meant that Ida wasn't looking at his bright red face. But very soon Riordan gave up on reaching the sky cow and ran zigzag after a butterfly.

"He's going to wear himself out," Kieran said, "and I'm going to end up carrying him back."

"You're a good brother," Ida said.

"Well, I'll be a better one when I go with Carrick," said Kieran, but as soon as he said it, he wished he hadn't. He didn't know for sure how soon—or if—the warrior would be back to get him. Perhaps on the next new moon.

"You went out to meet him? Do you have any idea where that will lead you? Why would you do that?" his mother asked.

"To show how well I could throw my spear. And my aim was perfect. I'll be a warrior."

"But you don't need to go with Carrick. You do well on the farm," his mother said. "Your family needs you. After losing your father, I don't want to lose you, too . . ."

"Well, our family needs a lot of things. If I go with Carrick, we'll be a lot richer." Kieran strode ahead. "Maybe we can even stay together—just the three of us!" Kieran's mother looked down. Kieran knew that everyone expected her to marry someone else. That's what widows did. The farmland was supposed to belong to Kieran and Riordan, but they weren't yet old enough to care for it alone. Providing food to Kieran's family was now their uncle's duty—so their uncle wanted their mother to marry again.

"But," Ida said, "I heard from a family across the river that their boy went, and Carrick didn't let him send anything back . . ."

"Are you saying our clan king's best man doesn't live up to his word?"

Ida and Kieran's mother looked at each other. "Kieran," his mother said, nearly whispering, "I'm not sure I trust Carrick. I heard that one of his men stole bread. Stole it from a family who needed it. When the father tried to get the bread back, Carrick stomped what was left under his boot and laughed! Your uncle can find someone else in our family to serve Carrick and the king. Not you."

Kieran thought about what it would be like to be one of Carrick's warriors. He had heard about the leader's strength. He was sure he could trust him.

"Wait until you hear what Patrick has to say. You might change your mind about Carrick," said Kieran's mother.

"Not likely," Kieran said. "I'm only going because Ida told me I could get a shield from him. Patrick isn't a warrior. He's probably giving these shields away because he doesn't need them. What does a priest know about fighting anyway?"

"You can think what you'd like, Kieran, but I've heard stories about Patrick," said Ida, stepping lightly. "He left his home and came here to Ireland to tell us about Jesus. He had a dream of voices from the woods of Ireland calling him here. He felt it in the depths of his heart."

The word "heart" made Kieran stop—and think of his own. He thought again of the question that led him to the crescent meadow the night he found the wolf pup. *What does your heart hunt for?*

As they got closer to the tiny wooden church, they saw a glorious, warm light coming from inside. They walked over the threshold onto rushes spread over the ground.

The building held only about twenty people. There were a few oak plank benches for older folks, but everyone else stood.

Kieran stared at two warriors, strangers. "Those are Dichu's men. He's the king of the clan that lives at the lake that joins the sea. They are traveling with Patrick," Ida whispered.

On a table at the front, the flames from three beeswax candles made one light. Where it was brightest, a man wearing bleached white clothes stood with his back to Kieran. He was speaking to a boy holding a lamb. Kieran thought the man's ginger-brown hair looked familiar, but he shook off the feeling. He should be looking around for shields.

The man wearing white bent down to dig out a pebble that was stuck in the lamb's hoof. Kieran thought this couldn't be the priest. He must be a farmer.

"It's Patrick," Ida whispered.

A woman said, "I'm sorry this boy has brought an animal into the church."

"It's fine," the man said. "This boy is a good shepherd, and I want to help him." His back was still turned, and he told the boy, "Tether your lamb outside. Come back here and say your prayers. Then, take your lamb to the high ground. Its foot will heal quickly."

The boy walked out with the creamy-white animal. Its face was so full of fluff, Kieran could hardly see its eyes. A girl even younger than Riordan rushed up to the man and showed him a tiny shamrock that grew inside on the floor of the church. "I've never looked at that kind of plant before in all my time in Ireland. It's beautiful!" The girl, smiling, ran back to her mother.

"Welcome," the man turned around and said. "Thank you for traveling to this humble church."

Kieran looked at him, astonished. Patrick was the man from the forest! The one who told him to go to the crescent meadow where he'd found Aisling! The one who had asked him the question about his heart that he wasn't sure he could answer . . .

12

"Peace be with you." Patrick looked straight at Kieran. He didn't feel peaceful. He wanted to find one of the shields he'd heard about and duck behind it. "What have you come here to find?"

"The love of Jesus."

"Answers to prayers."

"Peace in our hearts and homes."

Eager answers rang out from some of the women in the room.

Kieran found this all confusing.

Patrick nodded before saying, "There may be some here who are looking for a shield."

Kieran breathed out. How did Patrick know? Had Ida said something to him? At least it was something he could use.

Patrick continued, "The shield I have is a shield for your heart. It is a shield of love that protects you. Jesus loves you so much that he never stops loving you. His love surrounds you—above, below, in front, behind, to the right, to the left—every direction you can think of. It is the best shield you can imagine. A prayer shield that never fails you."

"A shield you can't see or hold?" Kieran said out loud. "That's useless, not real. You can't see or hold Jesus either then, right?" Everyone was looking at him. His mother was turning red.

Patrick walked right up to him. Kieran saw how his hands were rough. He had worked hard in his life. "Do you love something?"

Kieran thought of his mother, his brother, and the wolf. He was beginning to love the wolf. He thought too of his father, but that was the worst love of all, to love someone he'd never see again. It hurt because he was gone.

"Yes . . ." Kieran looked down.

"It's all right." Patrick put his hand on the boy's shoulder. "Is that love real, even though you can't see it? It is very real, isn't it?"

Kieran didn't answer, but he managed to raise his eyes a little as Patrick explained. "That is how this shield is real. When you believe in Jesus and have faith, he will give you this shield. You'll always have his love in your heart. You won't be afraid, and the path you take will be full of hope."

Patrick turned to the whole crowd, "Jesus loved us all so much that he died on a cross. He didn't fight back when soldiers came to take him to the cross. He chose something more courageous, to shield us from evil and death. But on Easter, he rose again from the dead. Now, if we follow him, we can have life forever in heaven."

But Patrick's words only reminded Kieran of his father's death after the battle, where even farmers like his dad were expected to fight. His mother didn't know that Kieran had looked into his dead father's eyes when they brought him back. They were as empty as caves, like those of the she-wolf hung over the hunter. There was no life in them.

Kieran knew his father was gone forever. Patrick, and Ida, and his mother may believe that souls lived on, but where? Up in the sky where his brother thought clouds were animals? Kieran felt he needed to get away. He slipped outside.

On the dusky walk home, Kieran kept a watchful eye, his sharp elbows always bent, ready to protect Ida, his mother, and Riordan from any danger along the way. The priest's words still drifted like smoke into his thoughts. Patrick's shield wasn't the kind he'd come for. But somehow Kieran felt a little surer of his steps. Could there really be such a thing as a shield of love? And could that love even include a wolf pup?

A SLIPPERY STUMBLE

13

Once home, Kieran couldn't wait to see the wolf pup. He had decided to bring some scraps of wool to Aisling to make her a cozier sleeping place. He kept them at the bottom of his sack. They were from the cloak his father had once worn. His mother had used the bark of an apple tree to dye the wool yellow. He also wanted to give Aisling some cold, leftover meat and maybe some buttermilk. As he ran toward her tree, he squinted. It was dusk and Kieran couldn't see her. . . .

He skidded on his knees and clawed at the ground, but he found only the white outline of the rope where he had tethered her. The loop was empty. Where had she gone?

He slapped the tether against his arm. He had feared it was too tight and loosened it, and now Aisling had slipped away. Kieran beat his fists against the ground. He had a sudden desire to call out to Ida. But could he trust her to keep the wolf pup a secret? No, it was better to keep this to himself.

Kieran thought of the clumsy way Aisling moved. She wouldn't be able to make her way in the world alone, not yet. He knew he had to find her.

But his father had always said he was better at running than tracking. Kieran frowned, but the memory helped him remember something useful. His father had once shown him how to use a tracking wheel.

Kieran picked up a stick and moved to a spot with damp earth. He drew a small circle with spokes coming out from its sides, like rays from the sun. He would go in the direction of each spoke, each in turn, to search for the pup. That is how he would keep track of the ground he had covered.

The first ray pointed back to the farms. Kieran followed this track, searching for paw prints, anything. If the little pup had gone there, a farmer would surely have killed her. Farmers feared that a pup would bring a pack of wolves. Those could kill cows, precious to the families there. Kieran breathed again when he didn't find any paw prints going to the farms.

He went back to the sun circle on the ground. The next two spokes led him to more and more trees. He had to keep trying. On the spoke opposite the farms, after a few paces, he saw a small shape in the mud. Kieran skidded on his knees to look. But the darkness was beginning to dull the outline just as it blurred the hard edges of the trees that stood silent. "Are you trying to hide her from me? Why don't you care?" he yelled at them.

Still, there was enough light to keep going. He stepped forward, hearing a voice he had not heard for a while. "Don't run when tracking," his father had always said. "Stop and listen."

Kieran paused and heard the river. He had never been able to hear it from this part of the forest before. It was too far away. *She was thirsty*, he thought. *That's why she ran away!* Kieran's heart knew that's where she had gone. He raced to the riverbank.

14

Above the damp air rising from the stream, the trees thinned. After one more step, he was close enough to fall in the gray water. There, the stream pushed broken reflections of the forest and sky, like fish, to a sea where Kieran had never been.

"Aisling?" Did she even know her name? But he couldn't call out "Wolf." Someone might hear.

"Aisling?" Silence. He looked down. Just because Kieran had decided to be her friend did not mean that she would be his.

Yip.

Could that have been her?

"Aisling?" As much as a howl could be quiet, he howled not like a large wolf but a small wind.

Yip, yip.

Down the bank, he saw a shape with a tail.

"Aisling," he said and yipped in return.

She ran toward him, but she came to a boulder that blocked the path. She turned toward the water. Aisling stepped on a branch to try to go round the boulder. It snapped and the little pup fell into a quick rush of water.

"Dad, help me!" Kieran tossed off his cloak and plunged in after the pup. Everyone had said his father swam like a fish, but Kieran had stayed out of the water since his father had died. With the current at his back, Kieran only needed to make sure he floated to begin catching up with Aisling. Baby eels, called elvers, slid fast by him.

The wolf pup splashed her paws and spun around in the water like a bubble. Kieran began moving his arms to catch up. Each time he lifted his head up, her downturned ears seemed closer and closer to the water.

"Swim to the rock in the middle!" It was closer than going back to the bank. Somehow, the pup seemed to understand. With strong arms, Kieran lifted his chest to see. The little pup's nose reached the stone. She put two paws up and wiggled to climb. Fast, cold water knocked her paws from the rock. She tried again and again, only to fall. Kieran could hear her terrified whimpers.

"I'm coming," Kieran called. But as he dove his head under, a broken tree branch arrowed toward his back. It snagged on his tunic and dragged him to three rocks in the river. Pinned there, he was far from Aisling.

Paddling, the pup stayed near her rock. Again and again, she put her front paws up, wiggled, climbed, only to slip down. Kieran could see her face dropping to the water. It seemed that she had stopped trying.

Kieran's tears dropped into the river. But then, he had an idea. He used his knife to rip his tunic that had twisted around the rocks. Like a fish, he wiggled out of the cloth. He didn't care as the tree branch scraped his back. Free, he swam his fastest ever.

He stretched and stretched his arms until at last near the small island, he felt Aisling's wet fur. When he gathered her close, she sank against his shoulder.

Kieran swam through rushing water until they came to a calm pool. "There is a well in the middle," he said to Aisling, "a spring coming up into the river.

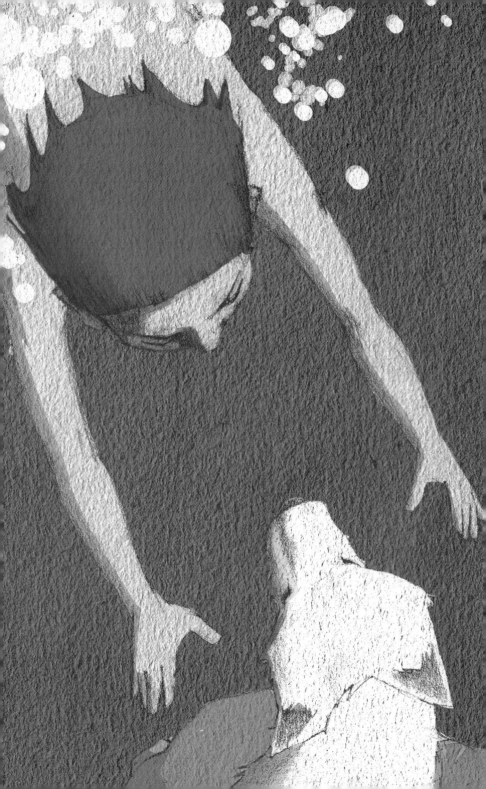

My father always told me this type of water is where the wise salmon lives. But it's not a place for wolf pups." He wondered where a place for wolf pups could be found.

He swam some more toward the shore. Willow trees on the edge made the river seem friendlier. Here, the stones knitted together in a solid road of safety.

Kieran set the pup down and she shook herself off and climbed onto his feet. After resting, Aisling spun around and around in happy circles. "Stay, okay?" He swam back to get what was left of his tunic. Back with the pup, he wrung it out and tried to use it to dry her. But her fur was thick, and the water rolled off the outer layer. After a while, the pup shook again and the last remaining drops went every which way. Finally able to rest, Kieran said, "You're lucky. With your fur, you have a shield with you all the time."

a slashing
attack

15

Back near his home, Kieran set the scraps of his father's cloak around the pup's feet. He touched the yellow strands his mother had woven in the cloak, and if he thought really hard, he could still see his father's face clearly.

He eased Aisling back into the tether, a collar around her neck, and watched her fall asleep.

"Could you watch over her?" he said, not quite sure who might be listening. But as he asked, a wind picked up and he shivered. As he headed home, Kieran wondered how long he could keep the pup. She had already escaped. But if she left again, there was no telling what could happen.

As he slept in his bed, nightmares filled Kieran's mind. Hunters with spears chased Aisling. Trapped in a stream, she spun away from him. A faceless person with a black club held her still body up as a red pool formed below.

Right before dawn, he woke up with his hands over his ears. He thought he'd heard the knife-sharp wail of a banshee. Kieran believed that banshee fairy spirits came to call out death. Would something die now? He thought he'd heard the same cry the morning before his father had died. Kieran looked into gray darkness outside. Mist, like cold blood, clung to his face.

Kieran couldn't eat breakfast. He checked to see that his father's broken shield was still under his bed. He collected some food and an ax and rushed to the forest. He felt a little better when he saw Aisling blink her eyes at him and squeak. But when he got close, Kieran could see that the tighter tether had notched a cut in her neck, and it was oozing blood.

Kieran felt he would be sick from a choice he didn't want to make. He said to Aisling, "I'm sorry. I can't take care of you well. You are cut today. Last night, you almost drowned. I don't want to, but . . . I have to hunt wolves again. Not to kill them. But to find any that might be left of your pack." He buried his face in her fur.

As drizzle began to fall, he hid Aisling in his cloak. "You're still so small that I think I run faster than you." Kieran set off. He stayed on the forest side out of the sight of his three cousins herding cattle to the river.

First, though, he wanted to take the pup to the stone in memory of his father. An old and wise man had scratched his father's name on the stone in Ogham, an alphabet for the Irish language. Kieran couldn't read it, but he had been told what it said. To show how his father had been rooted in their homeland, the stone listed the name of his grandfather and his and Kieran's clan.

The rain had pulled a gray cloth across Ireland's green. It had washed away the wildflowers his mother had left. Kieran knelt at the stone and found more blossoms. There, he saw something new—a twig cross she had made.

"This cross is about Jesus. But Dad didn't believe in Jesus. He had never heard of all of that. This isn't for him! Why would Mum put this here?" Kieran clenched his hands, confused. He was about to rip the cross out, but Aisling nudged him right by his heart. "Do you think it's all right, Aisling?" A feeling of peace draped over him like an extra cloak. He decided to leave the cross alone.

16

Moving on, they had not gone far when Kieran ran right into Patrick. Kieran spun around, trying to think of an excuse not to stop. If they stood around talking, Patrick was sure to notice the wolf pup stuffed in his cloak.

"Umm . . . let me just check this last tree for mushrooms." Kieran couldn't believe such a poor excuse had come out of his mouth. *Mushrooms? Girls would look for those!* He dashed behind a cluster of oak trees, quickly tethered Aisling, and eased her down. "Quiet."

"Are there many mushrooms around those oaks?" the priest asked.

"Yes."

"I have some meat I was given last night that I wish to give to you," Patrick said, holding out a parcel.

"I shouldn't take it." Kieran looked down unsure.

"You have a friend who needs it more than I do." Kieran took the offering slowly. "God gives us many blessings in this forest." Patrick bent down and started digging.

"You're looking for mushrooms, too?"

He smiled. "No, for a stone in the mud. Here is one. They're everywhere. I was like this stone, a stubborn one! It was stuck deep down and loved the mud just as the round pigs do."

Kieran laughed. Maybe this priest wasn't so serious after all.

"God, the Father, and Jesus, his Son—for they are one—in his kindness, lifted me up out of the mud like this rock." Patrick set the stone on a stump. "Even though I loved the mud, and did wrong things, and didn't even want to listen to him."

Patrick went on, "But when I was a slave, God said, 'Change your direction. Go on a new path.'"

"A slave?" Kieran had seen slaves at wealthy farms—boys who were tied up at night and forced to herd sheep during the day.

"Yes, a slave. And he told me to escape and run to find a ship."

"That's brave. But you could have died in a bog on the way." Bogs were muddy fields where people could get stuck or lost.

"That's what I thought! You see, we think alike. But God had lifted me out of the mud and given me faith. Because of faith, I listened to him and changed my path." He moved the stone in a different direction and even jumped it to a new stump.

"So when you got there, did they let you on a ship?"

"Yes, and I found my way home. But then, a new path opened. God asked me to come back to

Ireland, this time as a priest. My heart had been broken, but that is why it was open to what God was asking of me. I knew I had to follow this path."

"But weren't you afraid?"

"No, because I had the prayer shield of God's love. I prayed for Jesus to come with me. I asked that Jesus walk before me, behind me, above me, to the right of me, and to the left of me. God directed my path toward the good, and I feared nothing."

"The prayer shield! That's a good story . . . *for you*." Kieran heard Aisling digging. Making a big show of stretching his arms, he opened up his cloak a bit to block the view of the pup's oak.

"I think that God might be calling you, Kieran. Why don't you try the prayer shield for yourself? Ask Jesus to walk along with you. Perhaps to follow in the path of some small paw prints."

"Paw prints? What paw prints?" Kieran struggled not to look back toward Aisling. Had she stepped out? Was Patrick looking at her over the boy's shoulder at that moment?

Patrick smiled. "You should help any creature that needs help."

Kieran said, "Thank you for the meat."

17

Kieran looked back over his shoulder as he went to get Aisling, but Patrick had not followed. Did he know about her? Patrick wouldn't like wolves. Sometimes they killed lambs, especially weak or hurt lambs like the one he had helped in the church.

On the other hand, Patrick had smiled when he talked about paw prints. Maybe Patrick thought he should keep the pup. But what about Carrick? The warrior could return any day to get Kieran, and how would Aisling survive then? Kieran thought of how Patrick's stone changed direction. But that was just the problem. He wasn't sure which direction to follow forward, or how to find his way back to Aisling's den in the daylight.

Even though the dead she-wolf had likely been Aisling's mother, Kieran now wondered if the rest of Aisling's pack was near the den. She would be safer with them. But each step they seemed to get closer, he wanted to go home.

Aisling and Kieran walked together until they came to an ash tree. Its billowy bough of leaves made it look like a green cloud that might drift to another woods. They rested and shared some barley bread soaked in stew. Aisling whined and nudged him with her muzzle. She sniffed the air and took some steps away from the wind as it blew the steadying rain. Even though in his heart Kieran hoped she would have forgotten.

They came to the crescent meadow where Kieran had found the den. Aisling barked and ran ahead of him. Maybe she was running to her family!

"Aisling, wait!"

18

"Wait for me. Don't go in yet."

Aisling dove into the blackness of her old den. Kieran hesitated. If wolves were inside, they wouldn't understand that he had cared for her. He heard a growl. Could that be Aisling's family? No, the growl was too young. It was Aisling. Then, he heard a yelp. Something was attacking her. Another animal, not a wolf, had taken over the den!

Kieran didn't think. He shimmied into the den, his stomach sliding on the mud. From a flash of teeth came a strange, hissing noise. Charging heat blew from steaming breath.

He pushed his hand into black air and felt fur. He grabbed and pulled—his pup. A gray shape rushed toward them. Without any real aim, Kieran plunged his knife toward a high-pitched growl coming deep from the creature's belly.

Kieran backed out of the den where there was no cool air from nights before—only the heat of rage. He fell on his back. He set Aisling behind him and grasped for his ax. He had to swing it at whatever was following. A badger crashed into the daylight, and hit Kieran's face hard. Kieran threw as hard as he could. After the badger fell to the ground, Aisling whimpered.

The wet, warm feeling of blood ran down Kieran's face, and silence fell as the badger lay dying. Kieran reached for Aisling and searched the pup's fur with his hands. "Not hurt, not hurt. But I am," he said to Aisling. "The badger got me." Drops of blood fell from his face to the ground.

Aisling barked. Four tiny badger cubs had emerged from the hole and were nuzzling the large one he'd killed. The badgers' cave-rock eyes looked out from wide stripes. Just like Aisling, the cubs were now orphans. But this time, it was Kieran's fault.

Kieran held Aisling tight and ran back to the ash tree. He felt they'd been on the right path, but

Aisling's pack was gone. Wolves would never allow a badger to take over a den. Or had it been a badger sett all along? Where had the pack gone? If they'd left Aisling, he would have to find a better way to care for her.

Fluttering birds chattered over his head. "Be quiet. I need to think," he shouted toward them. There were too many questions he couldn't answer—questions Kieran didn't want to worry his mother with. He would go to Ida about his face. And as for Aisling, he wasn't sure.

A NEW DEN

19

After checking Aisling again for injury and finding none, Kieran tethered her in the forest. He pulled up the hood of his cloak and turned his hurt face away from the few people he met on the way to Ida's home.

Kieran climbed up the small dirt ridge that the men had long ago dug around the farm. A stick fence ringed the top. Ida's brothers had led their animals out to pasture, so the sheep and cattle pens were empty. A few huts held carts and tools. Her family had built the main house of woven twigs and mud, just like Kieran's, but it was larger. The thatched roof, an upside-down cone made of stems from cheerful yellow gorse flowers, guided all the rain down onto the ground outside.

Ida was checking on one of the lambs as the sun began to come out. As soon as she saw him, she asked, "What happened to your face?"

Kieran wasn't expecting her to ask so quickly. "Ran into a tree?" he added a questioning tone at the end of the sentence, though he had not meant to.

Ida stared at him for a moment. "Come with me inside. Everyone is away." Ida and her brothers lived with a foster family, friends of her parents. In Ireland, parents often sent their children to live with other families in order to build strong friendships.

Inside, Ida turned her back and spun around with her hands hiding something. "The secret healer." She opened her hands. "A puffball." A cloud of spores spewed out. "This mushroom will stop the bleeding."

Kieran began to doubt his decision to ask his friend for help. She dabbed the foul fungus on his wound. It felt like a giant worm. He tried not to sneeze from the puffing spores.

"Good." She took the moon-white mushroom away and opened a small box. She pulled out a palm-sized bowl and a wooden mallet.

"You don't need to hit me with that, do you?" Kieran joked. Anything was possible after the puffball.

"No, of course not." Ida smiled. She pulled some drying herbs hanging from the ceiling. "I grew these myself from seeds I found in plants at the edge of the forest. I planted them in a good patch of earth. Now they come in handy."

Ida mashed the herbs and wrapped them in a small scrap of cloth to make a pasty medicine. She reached up to hold it against his wound. Kieran heard steps outside.

"Someone's coming," Ida said. "Hold this against your face."

Ida's oldest brother came in. He grabbed a well-made spear. He nodded a brisk greeting to Kieran.

"A hunt?" Kieran asked, feeling his stomach sicken.

"Looking for wolves tonight," he said and left.

20

"I have to go," Kieran said.

"No, tell me what really happened. That's a slash mark, and unless trees have grown claws, you've been in some sort of fight."

"Ida, please, I have to go. They're hunting wolves again."

"Wolves. Did a wolf do this to you?" Ida asked worriedly. "They really *are* stalking our farms then. But you shouldn't go after them if you're hurt."

Kieran thought of Aisling waiting. "No! It wasn't a wolf." Ida looked at him with wide eyes and then looked down. "Please, Ida. I need to go right now."

Running to the forest, Kieran didn't try to hide the gash on his face. Where could he hide Aisling? If he climbed a tree, would she stay with him in it?

His heart pounded more with each tree he zigzagged around. *Please let her be all right,* he thought. What if the hunting party had already started scouting? Because he'd been gone, he hadn't heard about the hunt. Why had he been led on a path to the den when it had all brought disaster? Just then, Kieran heard a short, welcoming bark. He fell to the ground beside the pup. She nuzzled his face and began sniffing him because he smelled like a garden. As he gathered Aisling up, she growled. Was the hunting party nearby?

Kieran turned to see Ida gripping a tree trunk. She looked ready to climb it at any moment. Aisling bared her teeth, small but gleaming like spearheads. Kieran couldn't believe he'd let anyone track him. He thought that Ida moved like a shadow.

"Ida, it's all right." Kieran took a few steps back. "Don't look straight at her."

"That's not a dog," Ida said quietly, but fiercely. She grasped a low tree branch and scrambled part of the way up the sloping oak. A squawking gray jackdaw bird dive-bombed from the tree.

"Yes, it's a wolf. She is an orphaned pup."

"Drop her. She's going to bite you."

"The night they killed the she-wolf Patrick told me about a crescent meadow. That's where I found her."

"But why would Patrick tell you where to find a wolf? Wolves are dangerous. They sneaked near my mother's home farm when she was a girl and sniffed around the walls. They started howling like they were laughing at all the scared children. My mother never forgot it."

"Patrick was in the forest that night. He asked me what my heart hunted for. And then I found Aisling. Since then, I have been trying to protect her."

Aisling growled again.

"It seems she can protect herself," said Ida, digging her nails into the tree.

"Not from a hunting party."

"But she clawed your face. It's a bad cut."

"No. That was a badger. I thought the pack might have returned to their den. I wanted to take Aisling back to her family, but a badger had already moved in instead. I think I killed it. I don't know— Please don't tell anyone about Aisling!" Kieran nestled his cut face in Aisling's fur.

"Aisling? If you say so, I won't . . ." Ida climbed down from the tree, and Aisling lowered her tail halfway and laid her ears back. "If you want to protect her, though, you'll need to hide her from the hunting expedition tonight."

"I'll run deep into the forest."

"What about my family's farm? Maybe the granary where we store barley? No one would suspect a wolf to be near here."

"But bringing a wolf near cattle or farms on purpose is against the law. It's too risky. The worst part is that they'll kill her. Then, they'll say it's my fault for bringing a wolf pack too close. If anyone's cows are killed by wolves, my family will have to give them new ones. We aren't rich."

21

A horn rang out. The call for the hunt. There was no time to waste.

"We'll have to take our chances. *Come on*, Kieran," said Ida, her face scrunched and her usually big eyes squinting.

"You're right."

"Take my cloak to hide her."

"Yes, we can't just walk through a field carrying a wolf in plain sight." Kieran wrapped the little wolf in the cloak. She growled and pawed at it, but Kieran shushed her as the two hurried toward the granary near Ida's home.

Although Ida's brother, Alby, had taken the cattle out to pasture, an old cow was left behind. With a rumbling moo, she lumbered toward Kieran with a rusty bell clanking. A growl came from the cloak.

Ida grabbed the rope round the cow's neck and blew on a wooden whistle. "Grass. Grass. Come, old cow, and get some." She led the cow to the small pasture within the farm's fenced-in land.

With one hand, Ida pointed to the half-built granary. Coiled rope rings stacked on top of each other formed a tower half filled with barley. It was as tall as Kieran's shoulders. At the end of the harvest, Ida's brother would add more rings and the whole granary would be almost as tall as a tree. Kieran stretched to put Aisling in. Then he climbed up using each ring as a foothold. "But how do we hide? It's still open to the sky."

"Luckily, I already made the roof! I'll go get it." As Kieran waited, he arranged the cloak to hide Aisling. She buried her nose into his chest.

She nuzzled Kieran and started digging around in the barley. "Good. You like it. We may be here awhile." A grasshopper skittered out, and Aisling jumped on it, snapping her teeth and growling in delight.

But as Ida came back toward the edge of the granary, a horrible smell wafted up the tower. "Ida, what happened?"

"I'm spreading dung on the edges of the walls to hide the scent of the wolf."

She tossed up the cone-shaped roof. But he didn't expect Ida to climb up to the barley with them. This time, Aisling didn't even growl. Maybe she had liked the scent of Ida's cloak. They pulled the prickly roof over their heads.

"The sun is going down, but I can stay until my foster mother starts her night prayers. I pray with her," Ida said matter-of-factly. "Let's look out."

The rope rings let in breezes that helped clear the dung smell. Kieran peeked out and saw nothing of the hunting party and heard just one distant bark of a dog and an owl hooting. Ida shivered, and before Kieran could think too much, he pulled her cloak around her shoulders.

"Ida, what else do you know about Patrick?"

"He is brave. Patrick does kind things even when others don't agree. So I suppose he might want to help a wolf, too." She glanced at Aisling, and then added, "He once saved a fawn in Armagh." Armagh was a place in the north of Ireland not far from where Kieran and Ida lived.

"I guess he cares about animals."

"This is the story I heard. A man had given Patrick some land to build a church. The priest and his friends thought the church should look out over the green valleys from the highest hill. But when they climbed it, they found a deer and her fawn resting there."

"He and his friends were probably hungry."

"Yes, they'd been journeying for many days. Patrick's friends said, 'Let's kill the fawn and doe for dinner so we'll have more strength to begin building the church.'

"Patrick said, 'No, I can't allow this. The fawn has settled where we will place the altar of the church. That is the most holy part. We will spare her,'" Ida said.

"But they were hungry. It's hard to kill a baby deer—I've seen my uncle do it—but people have to eat." Kieran gathered Aisling in his arms and buried his face into her fur as he remembered the fawn he'd seen. Its spots were as light as sun dapples in the forest. He recalled that at the end of every hunt was a terrible stillness.

Ida clasped her hands together. "He said the fawn should live."

"What happened next?"

"He cradled the fawn in his arms and carried her down the hill."

"But she would have darted away from him. Fawns can disappear as fast as mist."

"The baby deer trusted him and rested in his arms, and the mother deer followed, just as people follow Patrick's words."

Kieran wondered if he should start trusting Patrick as much as the deer had. "I wonder if Patrick really would care for a wolf the way he protected the fawn."

"I don't know. . . . Some say wolves are evil creatures," Ida said. "But Patrick once told us that God cares for everyone, even his enemies. It is the same way you have cared for Aisling."

Kieran heard voices in the distance. "We should be quieter. Sorry." Aisling nestled in closer to Kieran's chest, and he felt peaceful. He had never had the chance to speak with Ida this way.

Before she left the granary, Ida prayed. "Jesus, stay with Kieran. Be his shield. Jesus, stay before him, behind him, above him, below him, to the right of him, and to the left of him."

Although the bits of reedy roof hanging down tickled Kieran's nose and made him sneeze, he soon fell asleep.

22

Howling woke him up. Aisling's howl! He grabbed her muzzle. "Quiet!" At first, Kieran couldn't remember where he was. Was he dreaming about being stuck in a tree? He strained to listen. Had anyone heard Aisling? Just when he felt safe, he heard a howl not far away. But it wasn't a real wolf's howl. The hunting party was howling to get wolves to call back. "No, Aisling." She whimpered, then settled down.

"In the farm right there! I heard a wolf right next to our ears!"

"This way!"

Kieran's heart beat faster as he heard the men's shouts. Would they find Aisling and kill her? He would be in trouble for bringing a wolf inside a farm. His family would owe crops and farm animals to everyone. Ida would get in trouble, too!

Kieran grabbed his knife so fast he almost scraped the sharp end. But he couldn't throw it at people from his own clan. He couldn't hide in the granary for much longer. His plan was to throw the roof, leap out when they wouldn't expect it, and run to the forest. Somehow Aisling must have understood because she made no sound. The men circled the rope rings.

The old cow stumbled over to the granary. She mooed with her mouth open but her eyes half-closed.

"This cow doesn't seem like she just saw a wolf," one of the men said.

"I heard the howl from here," another said. Kieran tensed his legs, ready to spring and fly over their heads when a soft song came along on the breeze. It was Ida, near the cow.

"Now young Ida, there are wolves about," a man said. "You'd best get away!"

"But our cow has had a limp. I'm here to check on her."

"We've heard a wolf howl."

"Maybe it was just a bad dream," Ida laughed. Kieran thought it was brave of her to make fun of the hunters. Ida shone an orange candle around the outside of the granary. "I don't see the glowing eyes of a wolf. Unless . . . you think one could climb?" She raised the lantern to the top of the tower.

What was Ida doing? She shouldn't lead the men to look up. They might peer inside and see him and Aisling. Many cracks in the rope rings and the roof could make them visible.

"Can wolves fly? I don't hear any growling or see any sharp teeth," Ida said and laughed, and thankfully Aisling made no sound. "Perhaps the wind and moon have played tricks on you, making you hear what has not sounded, making you see what has not shown itself."

Embarrassed, the men shuffled their feet. Pretending to be brave, one said, "Ida, you should be more careful. There are wolves . . . in the forest. Let's go back there."

"Thank you for protecting our farm," she told them. "You are all brave."

After they left, Kieran whispered a thank-you. As Ida turned, the candle lit her light reddish-blonde hair around her face. She winked and walked away.

THE FOREST

23

Kieran knew that he would have to teach Aisling how to hunt. She was getting bigger fast, and he couldn't find enough food for her on his own. With Ida's help and the shield prayer, he had kept her safe. In his mind, he knew he couldn't keep Aisling near him forever, but his heart wasn't ready. If one day he let her go, he knew he would probably never see her again.

He took the tether off her neck and ran a few steps away from her. The pup turned her head to the side and whimpered. Kieran ran back to her. "Follow!" he said, then ran several steps away. This time the pup scampered after him. "Good, good!"

Time went on. Aisling and Kieran loved running together. She broke a path, each swift move as smooth as the sun breaking open the day and night following it. Sometimes, they played so much that they almost forgot to hunt.

They came to a patch of clumpy bushes where Kieran knew there could be hares. He threw some rocks and one sprang up. "Go Aisling! Go! Hunt!" She turned her head to the side and ran forward, each foot like stones skipping across a pond. It didn't take long for her to corner and kill the prey. A raven made a clatter overhead. Kieran remembered the stories of how they followed wolves, sharing in their kills. But since its wingspan was almost as long as Aisling's body, Kieran waved his arms to make it fly away.

From the ridge to which it flew, Kieran thought he heard some wolves howling. That could be the song of Aisling's real family. He put his hands over her ears. He didn't want her to hear it and leave him. Seeming not to hear, she nuzzled him.

Just as Aisling didn't follow the sound of howling, Kieran didn't follow the calls of Carrick gathering boys for more tryouts. Whenever the warriors came near, Kieran ran deeper into the forest with Aisling. He couldn't leave the wolf just yet. But what would happen to his dreams of becoming a warrior?

Kieran and Aisling hunted together in the evenings after Kieran finished herding cattle with his cousins. Aisling always followed Kieran back to her favorite tree near the farm. Near it Kieran had dug a cozy bed in a small bank with soft, sandy earth. After eating, she'd settle down into her bed filled with scraps of cloth.

Kieran kept digging the bed wider as the wolf grew longer, becoming more of a wolf the clan would fear. But Kieran's love for her grew even stronger.

***

One day, Ida met Kieran at the edge of the forest. "How is the hunting training going?"

"Well. Six hares in six days. We chased a deer. But no luck there."

"But she always wishes to return here?"

"Yes. Any more talk of," Kieran began to whisper, almost as if Aisling might understand, "wolf hunting?"

"No, not since the men felt silly in my family's meadow." Ida smiled and jutted her chin out.

"Maybe even that prayer you said about 'Jesus before me' helped." He looked down at the ground.

"Prayer gives me courage to do the right thing," Ida said.

"I'm glad you think it's the right thing to help me and Aisling. Maybe if we're really careful, she can stay here forever."

24

A few days later, Kieran skipped home after some dawn hunting. With Aisling's help, his family was eating better than ever. But as he got closer, Kieran heard a voice he didn't know. A man, smiling and wearing a twig cross, came out of the hut. He turned and gave his mother a flower and waved goodbye. The man left without greeting Kieran.

The boy rushed inside. "Who was that?" he said.

"Kieran, have some stew for lunch," his mother said. "We'll talk later."

"No," Kieran said as Riordan played with stones in the corner. "What was that man doing here? Are you thinking about marrying again?"

"Kieran, sit down and have some food. He is a kind man, one who follows Jesus. He was only here to visit."

"I don't believe you!" Kieran shoved the wooden bowl off the plank table. It fell to the hut's floor and broke. It looked like the shattered shield under his bed.

Riordan shouted, "Dad made that! You broke it!"

Kieran froze—precious food wasted and a bowl his father had carved, now ruined. Kieran shouted,

"We can live here—just the three of us!" before he ran outside.

In the distance, Kieran saw the man calmly whistling to guide sheep. Reaching to the ground, Kieran found a pointy rock. As hard as he could, he threw it, aiming at one sheep on the edge of the herd. It startled and ran off course.

A rock whizzed toward him. Kieran dove into a ditch, but he was too late. Scraping and burning, a shard dug into his leg. It came from one of the man's friends.

He reached for another to throw. "No, Kieran." A rough hand caught his arm and brought it down.

"Patrick!" Kieran said. "If I had a real shield, it wouldn't have hit me. I saw it coming."

"It's wrong to throw stones to scatter the man's sheep."

Kieran wanted to hide his face. There was no excuse and almost nothing to say. "I know . . . I'm sorry . . . but I don't have to listen to you!" Kieran's mother came up to them, but Patrick waved her away.

"I know you want a wooden shield. I wish a shield like that could protect you from all of life's hurts. But what I can tell you is that Jesus is always here for you—even when you do something wrong.

Remember the prayer shield, Kieran. Jesus is with you no matter which way you turn. He is your shield."

"There is no prayer shield! I'm on my own. My father is dead. Now my mother may be marrying someone else. And I'm about to lose Aisling, my friend." Kieran didn't say any more about that.

Patrick said, "Jesus can help you and your friend. He loves all of us and wants to be our very best friend. That is why your mother loves Jesus, Kieran, and why she was baptized."

"My father didn't know about Jesus. He wasn't baptized. And he didn't need any help. He took care of his family himself!"

Patrick picked up a stone covered in mud. He brushed it off with his hands and held it up to the rain that had begun to fall. "I'm sure your father was a good man, Kieran. It's right that you want to be like him. But perhaps you have your own path to follow. When a person is baptized, a whole new life opens up in front of him."

"I need to take care of my family. That's what my father would want. But I'll be one of Carrick's warriors. That way I'll get more cattle to help my mother and brother."

"Is that what you think following Carrick will bring you? More cows? I'm not so sure."

Kieran looked into Patrick's concerned face, but then looked away.

"Your family needs you here, caring for them," Patrick said. "And what about the animal you told me about?" Kieran felt tears in his eyes so he turned and walked away. He didn't want Patrick to see them.

When he returned to his family's hut a while later, his mother was not there. He found her and Riordan in the rundown hut where Carrick's warrior had demanded some bread. Patrick was leading a prayer inside. Ida and his mother were mashing some herbs in a bowl, and another woman placed a damp cloth on a woman's head. She was lying down and seemed sick. Patrick made a cross shape in the air and the sick woman's young daughter cried. Kieran wasn't sure what to think—or what to do.

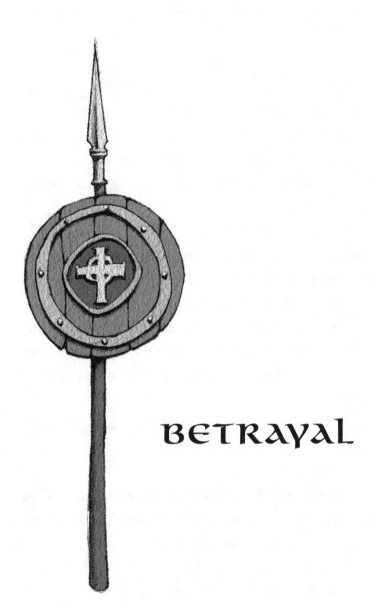

BETRAYAL

25

A few weeks later, Kieran and Aisling went on one of their hunts. Kieran trailed behind Aisling as they ran through a small meadow. "This is all the green of the whole world!" Pale green shamrocks grew from dark soil. Moss grew between dirt pockets amongst rocks.

Aisling's legs had begun to thin out like strong branches of pale ash trees. She had become almost as big as Kieran, and now he always fell behind her as she slipped through the forest.

Kieran stopped to rest and lean on a tree. Aisling still streaked ahead after a rabbit she had flushed from some brush. Kieran breathed fast; he couldn't catch up.

"Aisling!" he finally yelled. He walked to a pond where the haze of dawn still hung over the water.

"Aisling?"

Kieran heard howls in the distance. Had Aisling heard them first? It seemed there were other wolves nearby. He didn't know what he would do if the wolves decided to attack Aisling. He crept toward the sound without snapping twigs.

Kieran came to a break in the trees in sight of a grassy area along a small ridge. He squinted in the sudden sunrise and looked up. He could see misty gray shapes running. Wolves. They reached the top of the ridge, and Kieran gripped the trunk of a young tree. The pack jumped and played, but one of the wolves took a few steps down the hill and stared toward Kieran.

The one wolf was Aisling. As the pack left over the crest of the ridge, Aisling barked. Kieran took one step to follow. Then she turned and, like mist, vanished over the top.

Kieran slammed his fist into the tree. "You've left me? Just like that?" he yelled. He rushed to the hill to try to find her tracks. But a sudden wind kicked up and erased the places the grass stalks had bent over. The path was gone.

Kieran sunk to his knees. *We were friends*, he thought, *weren't we?* He had fed her, protected her, and taught her to hunt. But he couldn't be like her own family.

For a moment, Kieran wished he was a bird— even a raven—though he didn't like them. In just a few wing beats he'd be able to see if Aisling was all right.

Kieran knew he could keep running over ridge after ridge, but at last he would end up at his clan's boundary. If he crossed it, warriors from another clan could attack him. Or worse, he might stumble into a bog. Only those who knew the paths of higher ground could pass safely through the mucky, marshy land.

As Kieran turned from the place where Aisling left him, he felt his spirit had gone with her. He couldn't see or hear her anymore. The wolf pup was another thing he had loved that now was gone. There was no Aisling, no shield, no God called Jesus, no love that stayed with you always. He felt nothing around him at all.

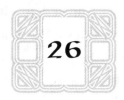

26

Back home, Kieran didn't want to talk to anyone. He looked at his mother sideways and mumbled a greeting.

Riordan, scared, ran toward the hut. "Hide! The mean warrior is here," he said.

"Carrick? Are you sure?"

Just then, boys began running to meet at the center of the farms. *It must be Carrick!* Kieran thought. Aisling was gone; there was nothing keeping him from joining Carrick and helping his family now. He wondered whether he should go back to Carrick and try to impress him again. Once may not be enough. Carrick would want to know he could do more than just throw a spear.

The boys gathered in a circle around the tall and broad-shouldered warrior leader. "It's a race," they said as they punched each other's arms. They all began to gather in a mob at some starting point, but Kieran had arrived late and was at the back. His legs felt like stones from trying to keep up with the wolf. Ida's stocky brother, Alby, stood ready at the front. Kieran wondered if she was watching.

There was so much noise Kieran couldn't hear the signal to start. He didn't know where to run or finish either. Kieran just ran. Legs burning, he passed some younger boys at the first turn.

Kieran could still see Alby's ginger hair up ahead. He remembered how when they'd thrown spears, Alby's had ditched in the dirt. But in a race, Alby could use his height and long legs to stay ahead.

Not wanting to lose, Kieran pushed off more with his feet. All the days of running with Aisling had made him stronger. He pulled ahead of the two boys directly behind Alby. They were already rounding the corner. *It's not fair*, he thought. Alby had started way ahead of him, but now Kieran had the chance to surprise him.

Kieran ran closer and launched his arms forward with all the anger in his heart at losing Aisling. As Kieran shoved past, Alby fell face forward onto the ground. Kieran jumped over him and ran alone to Carrick.

"Well done!" Carrick exclaimed. "My men don't let anything—or anyone—get in their way."

Kieran had won the race, but as he stepped out of the crowd that gathered around him, he saw Ida's face. In that moment, he knew that he had lost something important.

27

Kieran tried to find her, but he ran into Alby first. He made fists, thinking there would be a fight. Alby was bound to be angry. "I wouldn't try hitting me, Alby," Kieran warned. "I'm faster. I'll surely win." Kieran was looking for a place to punch Alby and noticed the twig cross on the boy's chest, much like his sister's.

"I suppose I could hit you, but I won't. I don't care about joining up with Carrick or winning the race. He won't pick me anyway. I just love to run."

Kieran was confused. "You *should* fight me . . . I knocked you over . . ."

"But we've always been friends," Alby replied. "What happened today, Kieran? What's wrong in your heart?"

The question startled Kieran.

"Maybe you should go and find Ida," Alby continued. "She's probably more angry with you than I am."

"I don't know what to say . . . I'm sorry . . . I'll find your sister."

On legs that felt like old tree branches at the bottom of a muddy bog, he went toward Ida's house. He watched as the girl's foster mother placed their best wheat bread, a wooden pot of honey, some of the shamrocks Ida liked to collect, and a shining green stone in a sack. Without a glance his way, Ida turned and left.

"Ida! Ida!" Kieran trailed after her. She walked into the sun and didn't turn to look at him. Legs aching, he ran again to overtake her.

"I guess I shouldn't try to beat you running," Ida said, her eyes squinting. "Maybe you'll knock me down, too. Go away. I have to take this gift to

Patrick." The trees beside them rustled. Squawking birds flew out.

"I'm sorry, Ida. It was—It was a chance to impress Carrick. Everything is fair in a battle."

"A battle? Within our own clan, and against my brother who you've known all your life? What's gotten into you?"

"I told Alby I was sorry. I was angry. Aisling is gone. She's run away."

Ida looked away. "She is? Gone where?" Bits of dandelion fluff floated between the two of them.

"With other wolves, her pack . . ."

"I'm sorry she's gone, but please leave me alone. What you just did to my brother was wrong."

Kieran said, "Just let me explain."

"Not now. I'm on my way to see Patrick. I'll find peace once I've seen him."

"I'll never find peace until I find Aisling. Now I'm losing you as a friend, too."

"I'll be able to forgive you, Kieran, some day." She sighed. "But right now, I need some peace. Patrick always helps me find it and discover the best path for my life."

"Maybe Patrick can tell me what path Aisling took. Patrick helped me find her in the first place. He may know where I should go to look for her now."

"I'll ask Patrick about Aisling. But today I'm going alone. I can't wait until Patrick sees this well-made food and especially this green stone." Again, there was rustling in the shrubs nearby.

Kieran had no choice but to let her walk away. What was the best path for a life anyway? He had felt lost until he found Aisling. Now that she was gone, he felt lost again. Perhaps Aisling was where she belonged—with other wolves. Perhaps he needed to leave this place like she did to join Carrick. He sat down on the ground and put his head in his hands.

28

Two horsemen sped through the meadow like clouds shadowing a lake on a windy day. Fear spread quickly from his heart out to his shoulder blades. Kieran started to run—first to Aisling's old bed. As he got closer, he saw some twisting leaves. *Perhaps she's back, maybe digging after some grasshoppers*, he thought hopefully. But no, as he slid to his knees, a rabbit bounded away.

He cut through the forest, drenched in the late morning sun. Close to the road, he saw Ida looking at bluebells. As a breeze stirred the dusky blue flower tops, Kieran heard the sound of hooves. They didn't beat at the pace of a farmer eager to get home at the end of a long day. No, someone was urging his horse on too fast.

"Ida, let's drop down to the forest."

"Kieran?"

"Ida, drop back down now!"

"Why?"

The horseman was already upon them.

As Kieran raised his eyes to try to see the horseman's face, the rider hit him with a shillelagh. He opened his mouth for breath but could feel nothing. It seemed the clouds were drawing up all the air of the world.

"Kieran!"

No, he thought. He wanted her to run! The black horse whirled around and pawed the ground.

"So, who's this?" The hooded man's face was covered, except for his eyes that he narrowed at Ida.

Kieran wondered when or if he had heard that voice before. As he tried to sit up, his ribs jabbed at him with sharp pain. The man jumped off his horse in one practiced motion and strode toward Ida.

"Give me the sack. It should go to the clan king—not some muddy priest. Hand it over."

She turned toward the forest, her foot crushing bluebells before he grabbed the back of her dress. The man dragged her back.

Kieran reached for his hunting knife, but it wasn't there. He looked around so fast the world spun.

Where had he lost it? Kieran turned toward the forest to the glow of orange eyes.

The wolf rushed to the path without a sound. The fur around her neck stood up. Her ears tipped forward. Her eyes stared only at the man. Aisling!

"Aisling, get him. He's hurting us." The wolf charged.

The black horse reared and whinnied. The man shoved Ida toward the wolf. Meaning to flee, he ducked the slashing hooves and lunged after his horse. With the horse stunned, he jumped up and rode away.

Ida lay in front of Aisling. The wolf ran a few paces toward the path the horse had taken, but it was gone. She circled back and nudged the girl. Then, she ran to Kieran.

"Ida!" Kieran yelled. Ida began to sit up, brushing dirt off her face. She looked down at the ground. "Jesus protect me," she said. "Jesus with me. Jesus above me—"

Kieran said, "Are you hurt?" Ida didn't answer. She was still praying. "He's gone. Aisling will attack him if he comes back." Kieran hugged the wolf. *If not for her . . .* he thought. "Ida, are you all right?"

"Jesus behind me—I want to go home!" Ida said.

Kieran heard hooves striking the ground from the other direction. "Hide!" Ida sat there still stunned. "Hide." He grabbed her hand and yanked her to the woods. Aisling plunged into still deeper shadows.

THE SAINT'S PATH

29

Kieran couldn't trust any traveler after what had just happened. But as the horse approached, he could see it was Patrick, wearing his simple cloak and guiding his mare gently.

"It's Patrick," said Kieran. "Maybe he'll go with us back to our farms."

"No," said Ida. "I can't see anyone now."

"But Patrick can help make sure you're safe," said Kieran. He didn't know what to do.

"Peace be with you," said a warm, but strong voice behind him. "I've just come from my prayers. Let me guide both of you home." Somehow Patrick had seen them in the trees. Although she had started to cry, Ida followed him back up to the path. Kieran tried, but couldn't help lift her up to the tall horse. The pain was too much.

Along the road home, Kieran told Patrick what had happened—but not the part about the wolf.

"You were sent here to help Ida, just like I was sent to help the two of you now. We are all Jesus' hands and feet here on earth to help each other. Jesus is always helping us even when we may not know it." Kieran thought about how he had helped Aisling, and how she had helped them by driving off the horseman.

When Patrick asked about who the attacker could have been, Kieran couldn't say. He had never gotten a clear look at his face. He didn't think he knew the man's voice either.

Kieran said, "Thank you for guiding us back safely."

"You are welcome," replied Patrick. "But all I have done and can do is from God. I've never really been the one guiding you. God has—by working through me and speaking to your heart."

As they neared their farms, they heard excited shouts and even a horn blowing.

A hunt?

A man they knew rushed toward them. He shouted, waving his arms to Kieran, "A snarling wolf is on the loose. It attacked a traveler on the path. He says that a boy commanded it."

Kieran felt sick. He could barely breathe because of his ribs. He spun toward Aisling's old den.

A mob rushed toward them. "There! There!"

Kieran turned to look behind him, his ribs hurting with the twist. On a small rise before the break of trees stood Aisling, fangs showing.

The group of men parted as a black-clad figure strode forward. His hood was now off. Before Kieran could bear to look at the man's face, he saw a torc. *No, it couldn't be.* Kieran looked up and saw Carrick's glinting green eyes.

"That boy can't be trusted," Carrick pointed at Kieran. "He orders that wolf around." Aisling growled as the fur around her neck ruffled.

"That wolf is going to attack us all. Kill it!" Carrick gripped his club. Some of his men began to draw back spears.

"No! Run, Aisling!" A wolf could outrun almost anything. But Aisling stood still. Her fur blew in the wind like grass in a meadow. Kieran ran to stand in front her. "If you strike her, you must strike me!"

30

"Kieran, get away from the wolf!" Kieran's mother shouted as she grabbed the back of Carrick's cloak. He shoved her to the ground. Riordan darted out from behind some shrubs and kicked Carrick's leg. Kieran gripped his knife, and Aisling showed her teeth.

"Back away," Patrick said. *Did Patrick think he was wrong, too?* thought Kieran. But Patrick was telling Carrick, not Kieran, to back away.

Patrick raised his hand out in front of him. "This wolf is God's creature. It hasn't hurt anyone."

"It would have torn me to pieces on the road." Carrick pointed toward the wolf. "And that boy commands it."

Not taking his eyes from Carrick, Patrick walked backward toward Aisling. The wolf closed her jaws and her ears moved back. Patrick took some meat from his bag, bowed to the wolf, and laid it at her feet.

"Look, the wolf is calm," Kieran's mother said. "It won't hurt anyone."

"Kieran has cared for this wolf since she was orphaned," said Patrick as he petted Aisling's head. He turned to Kieran, "You have a strong faith to make friends with an animal other people fear."

"I said that wolf would've killed me out on the road." Carrick raised his club toward Patrick.

"Stop, Carrick," someone in the crowd said. "That's a holy man. You may come to regret it you if you lay a hand on him."

"Perhaps you need to find a new road home," Patrick said, putting his hand up to Carrick. "Why don't you walk with me for a while?"

"But you walk with Dichu's men." Carrick spat at Patrick's feet. "No friends of mine."

"Isn't there a saying on this island, 'The mountains never meet, but two men can always speak'?"

An older man in the crowd said, "My grandfather always said that. It's old wisdom."

Almost whispering, Patrick told Kieran, "Take Aisling to the west edge of the lake. You will find a wooden plank leaning on a willow. Cross the lake with your wolf on that raft."

Ida nodded to Kieran.

"God gives this creature the safe haven of the woods," Patrick told the crowd. "Let us all bless this wolf on her journey away from here." He pulled a silver bell out from his sleeve and rang it. Kieran and Aisling slipped away.

THE LAKE

31

As Kieran and Aisling gazed at the calm surface of the lake, Kieran thought of his mother's bravery, speaking out to protect Aisling. He smiled to think how his brother, Riordan, who had always been so scared of Carrick, darted from nowhere to kick him.

Aisling howled.

"Quiet," Kieran whispered before adding, "thank you for coming back to rescue us, Aisling. I guess I didn't really lose you after all!"

He didn't hear anyone behind him. Did Patrick really keep Carrick and the rest of his men from following?

"I'll look for the plank Patrick said would be here," Kieran thought aloud. "But I don't know how such a thing can cross the water." Despite the pain, he moved around tree after tree and scared a mouse. Finally, he came to the last place he could think of, a rusty willow with long leaves. Leaning on the trunk of the tree was a large, wooden circle.

"A shield!" Kieran shook his head, not believing. "At last, a real shield made of wood." He walked it to the bank. "But now I need a boat," he said to Aisling.

Kieran heard a horn blow in the distance—hunters gathering. It was a sound to run from. Aisling ran back and forth along the shore, and Kieran looked to the sky. He hadn't thought there was a heaven. But Patrick seemed sure enough. He felt stronger.

Kieran cast his arm, pointing to the other side of the lake. It was too far away for them to see it. "Swim there," he ordered the wolf. "Go!"

Aisling paced along the water's edge. The horn sounded again. Kieran pulled off his boots and waded in. "Swim there." He cast his arm. But Aisling only waited. Patrick had told him to float to the other side of the lake on the plank. Kieran couldn't imagine how that could be possible. Still, what else could he do but try?

Kieran floated the shield on the edge of the waves. It drifted back up to the shore. "See, there's no way." The horn sounded closer. Aisling nudged at the far edge of the wooden shield. As Kieran pulled it into the lake, the shield rose up out of the mud and headed into deeper water.

"Jesus before me!" Kieran cried out, remembering the prayer shield. Kieran dove toward the floating shield, swam, and climbed on. But there was no room for a wolf, not now that Aisling had grown.

The plank began to stream out to the center of the lake. "Aisling!" The wolf splashed at the water's edge. "Aisling, follow! Follow me." Without a glance to the forest beyond, the wolf left the shore and swam a straight path into the lake behind Kieran.

As they reached the center of the lake, the trees dropped out of sight and the sky seemed stitched to the water all around. The shield stopped moving straight and started to go around in spirals. Kieran laughed at the spinning feeling. Aisling paddled in place. But as Kieran kept whirling, the wolf's face was sinking closer to the surface of the water.

"Enough fun," he said to himself. "We need to get to the other side." He had to guide Aisling to the other shore. She was growing more and more tired. Still, the plank drifted in a spiral. Kieran's heart beat faster. He couldn't stay here. "How can I steer this?" Kieran asked aloud. He looked down at the water.

Would he have to let go of the shield and swim?

32

The lake's murky waters looked even darker than the den where he had first found Aisling. Just then, the sun came out from behind a cloud and he could see his reflection. He had never seen his own face so clearly. *My eyes are as dark as this lake—just like my father's.* Surrounded by water, Kieran thought of what Patrick had said about Jesus and baptism—all his father had not had the chance to hear.

Could it be that my path is to follow Jesus? he wondered. *One thing I know: Aisling's path is in the forest, and I need to let her go. This time, I will be happy for her instead of feeling sorry for myself.* His heart felt at peace.

The plank stopped its spiral and turned straight toward the other shore. "I can stay on the shield!" he yelled. Aisling seemed to find new strength, too. Kieran knew they would be all right when he saw Patrick step out from among the trees.

When they landed on solid ground, Kieran buried his cheek into the wolf's damp shoulder. At that edge of the lake, flags of mist-white bog cotton waved from green stems to welcome them.

But the best welcome came from Patrick. "I rode my horse here," Patrick said, smiling. "She's faster than a floating shield. I knew that you would make it across!"

Kieran was ready to set the wooden shield down. But he heard a horse running in the forest.

"It's Carrick!" Kieran led Aisling behind some bushes. "Stay here," he told her. Patrick took a step toward the sound, but Kieran took two. "I'm not afraid," the boy said, gripping the wood until his hand hurt.

"Remember that I'm here to help," Patrick said. "I'm always your friend."

33

Carrick jumped down from his horse and stepped to the edge of the lake. "Put your shield down. I'm not here to fight you, boy. I have an offer for you."

Kieran kept the shield across his heart. "You attacked me, my friend on the road, and Aisling, my wolf."

"The girl?" Carrick said, "I couldn't see what clan she was from. I had a hood on to keep the dust of the road out of my eyes. I'm sorry. But when I saw your wolf, of course, I tried to kill it. Wolves are dangerous to everyone. I never knew a wolf and a boy could work together."

Carrick went on, "Your name is Kieran, right?" The boy nodded cautiously. "Well, Kieran, I've been thinking. If you can command a wolf, you could be very useful. With a wolf helping us, the enemy clans would be too scared to attack us."

"What are you saying? That I could still go with you? That I could keep Aisling with me?" Kieran asked. Everything became unclear again.

Patrick stood behind Kieran, ready to protect him. He remained silent but held his hands out in prayer.

"First, we'll take revenge on the clan that killed your father. And I'll give your family a cow today. If you and your wolf join us, no one else's men will be stronger. No one will ever steal from our clan again."

Carrick smiled and patted Kieran on the back. "Come along! You and your family will be rich. And with that beast at your side you'll be one of our strongest warriors, maybe even their leader once I'm too old. But you'll need a better shield than that! Don't worry! The shield I give you will have bronze on it, too."

Kieran turned and looked at Patrick and his mind filled with memories. Kieran remembered looking for the crescent meadow and sleeping next to Aisling the night he found her. He thought of how happy Aisling was after he rescued her from the river, and how Ida had given him medicine for the cut on his face. Then Kieran remembered the warrior who had taken food from a poor farmer and how Carrick had tried to steal Ida's stone. He thought about his family and his father's broken shield. But one thought was the clearest, Patrick's question. *What does your heart hunt for?*

"No, Carrick," Kieran said. "I don't want to steal. There is another way to be strong, and I've found a shield that is stronger than any you have. I don't want to be one of your warriors anymore."

"Aisling was made to run free in the forest," Kieran went on. "I don't want her to kill men and die with a spear in her heart! You are a strong man, Carrick, and good at getting others to follow you. Imagine if you tried doing good things instead of bad ones?"

Carrick clenched his fists. His face turned red. "That is your answer?" he yelled. "I won't forget this!" With three quick strides, he reached his horse, mounted, and left.

Patrick said, "Kieran, you spoke so well."

Kieran smiled wide. He smiled even wider when he saw Ida run from a patch of willows, but this scared him, too. He said, "Ida, what are you doing here? You should never have come here!"

"I was running to warn you that Carrick was following you. But I couldn't catch up. Please tell me Aisling is all right."

Kieran turned around to see the wolf stepping out from behind the brush. He hugged her. "We are far from Carrick and the hunters now. But Aisling, you need to find a home in the forest. That's where you belong."

Kieran whispered only to the wolf, "I'll miss you. This time, though, I won't be lonely or afraid."

Kieran ran forward to the forest, but Aisling ran ahead and then back to him. Again, he ran forward, but she circled back. On the third time, Patrick said, "God has directed our path toward what is good, and we fear nothing." Then, the wolf, the tips of her fur gold in sunlight, streaked ahead through gray trees. She was gone.

Kieran held up the wooden shield. "This shield isn't big enough to protect everything my heart loves. Can I trade it for the prayer shield you told me about instead?"

Patrick smiled. "I've been waiting for this, Kieran! You have courage to follow your own path. You'll have to enter the water again, but this time it won't be a lake."

"Water?" asked Kieran. "But I'm already soaking wet!"

Patrick laughed. "The next step of your journey is baptism. Then, Jesus will be with you everywhere and always."

"Yes, Patrick," Kieran said. "I want to follow Jesus."

"You are welcome to come along and pray with me always."

"And me! Thank you for helping me on the road," Ida said.

"I will always help you," Kieran said firmly. "You would never have been there alone if I hadn't been so mean to Alby."

"It's all right. I forgive you," Ida said.

Kieran looked up. On a rocky crag in the distance, he could see Carrick kneeling next to his horse. Silent and still, he had bowed his head. His hands covered his face.

"Look!" Kieran said.

Patrick gathered the children close. "In time, an enemy can become a friend. Jesus can forgive everyone. He loves even men like Carrick."

Kieran set the wooden shield down. He picked up some stones and skipped them across the water. They made quick shapes like wolf-pup paw prints, glittered, and faded to one path of light.

hISTORICAL NOTE

There are many wonderful legends about Saint Patrick, but his true life story of escaping slavery and bravely returning to Ireland is just as exciting. Patrick lived in the fifth century and was born at the edges of the Roman Empire. Historians are not quite sure about his exact birthplace, but it could have been in the north of England or Scotland. He wrote the story of his own life while on a mission to bring Christianity to the people of Ireland.

Although the story of Kieran and Aisling is fiction, wolves did live in Irish forests at that time. Patrick would have been likely to reach out in a compassionate way to a boy who was struggling to find the right path for his life.

Sadly, wolves no longer live in the wild in Ireland. People who feared that wolves would kill their cattle hunted them to extinction on the island.

Saint Patrick's famous feast day is on March 17. On that day, the author of this book invites you to celebrate and search for paw prints for a new path in your life, and let the shield of prayer be your guide, too.

SAINT PATRICK'S PRAYER

Saint Patrick's famous prayer is known by many different names. Some call it "Saint Patrick's Lorica," others "The Breastplate of Saint Patrick." In this book, it was called "the prayer shield." It is a beautiful prayer about journeying with God's love and protection that we can pray today. Here is part of it.

Christ with me, Christ before me,
Christ behind me, Christ in me,
Christ under me, Christ over me,
Christ to the right of me, Christ to the left
    of me,
Christ in lying down, Christ in sitting, Christ
    in rising up,
Christ in the heart of every person who may
    think of me!
Christ in the mouth of everyone who may
    speak to me!
Christ in every eye which may look on me!
Christ in every ear which may hear me!

DISCUSSION QUESTIONS

1. What would you do if you found a wolf pup like Kieran did?

2. Which character in this story do you think is most like you? Why?

3. When did you feel most scared about what would happen to Aisling? In the river, with the badger, at Ida's farm, or at the end when Aisling fought Carrick? How do you think Kieran felt? What do you do when you are scared?

4. Why was Kieran confused and disappointed when Patrick's shield turned out to be Jesus' love and a prayer? How did Kieran feel about Patrick's prayer shield at the end of the story?

5. Think about what might happen after the end of the story. What will Kieran and Ida do next? Where will Aisling go? What will Carrick do?

6. Each friend in the story had special gifts to share. Kieran was able to hunt, track, and swim to protect Aisling. Ida was able to heal wounds and knew when to pray. What do you think your special gifts are? How can you share them with those around you?

7. Kieran became courageous and faithful by caring for a wolf pup. In your life, is there a grandparent, parent, brother or sister, friend, neighbor, pet, animal in your backyard, or garden needing your care and help? Write a paragraph or draw a picture about that person, animal, or thing in nature.

8. How did you feel when Kieran pushed Alby down in the race? Have you ever been tempted to do something mean to someone in order to impress someone else?

9. How do you think Kieran felt when Aisling finally left him? What should you do whenever you feel alone or sad?

acknowledgments

I am grateful to my daughter, Laura, the reason I started writing. I wish to thank my husband, Michael, who always goes along as I take many notes about obscure flowers, animal tracks, rocks, or other things I find inspiring for stories or poems.

I've never forgotten my love of children's books, perhaps because they were such a part of our happy family when I was young. My mother, Cheryl Weaver, an elementary school teacher, put stars on a poster for the books my sister, Kristi, and I read. My father, Kelly Weaver, loved to quote poetry, adding to the literary heritage that so inspires me now.

sherry weaver smith

became Catholic after working alongside Salesian Sisters who were dedicated to helping homeless and working children in Manila, the Philippines. After marrying her husband, Michael, Sherry wrote her first poems and children's fiction for their daughter, Laura. Sherry's haiku collection, *Land Shapes*, has been published by Richer Resources Publications. Sherry has also worked in various product management and grant-writing positions for healthcare companies and nonprofit organizations. She received her bachelor's degree from Duke University in math and East Asian studies, and a master's in politics from the University of Oxford, England. *The Wolf and the Shield* is Sherry's first adventure with Pauline Kids.